The S[...]

Mystery

Abandoned
Lighthouse

Written by
Suzanne Grant Perdew
and Grant Perdew

Book 12
Created by
Jerry D. Thomas

Pacific Press® Publishing Association
Nampa, Idaho
Oshawa, Ontario, Canada

Edited by Jerry D. Thomas
Designed by Dennis Ferree
Cover and inside illustrations by Stephanie Britt

ISBN 0-8163-1819-0

00 01 02 03 04 • 5 4 3 2 1

Contents

Other Books in
The Shoebox Kids Series

This is the last book in The Shoebox Kids series. But don't worry! Look for the new *Shoebox Kids Bible Stories* at your Adventist Book Center or at <www.adventistbookcenter.com>.

Hi!

Have you ever seen a lighthouse beaming its light to guide ships away from dangerous rocks? Have you ever been inside a lighthouse? A lighthouse can be a very interesting place to visit if you're at the beach or the seashore. Keep your eyes open for one the next time you take a trip.

The Shoebox Kids are back! The same kids you read about in *Primary Treasure* are in their twelfth book. This time, Maria and Chris and their family are on vacation at the seashore. Besides living in a yurt, Chris and Maria find a mystery when they discover an old cemetery. And that mystery leads them to an abandoned lighthouse and the story of the lighthouse keeper.

The Mystery of the Abandoned Lighthouse is a special Shoebox Kids book. It's the only Shoebox Kids book written by a kid—Shoebox Kids reader and primary Sabbath School member Grant Perdew—and his mother Suzanne Perdew. The story they share shows us the importance of trusting others and the difference God can make in your life.

Reading about Chris and Maria and the other Shoebox Kids is more than just fun—it's about learning what being a Christian really means—at home, at school, or on the playground. If you're trying to be a friend of Jesus', then the Shoebox Kids books are just for you!

Can you solve the mystery of the abandoned lighthouse before Maria and Chris do?

Jerry D. Thomas

1

The Mystery Begins

"Why are we stopping here?" asked Chris, as the Vargases' car pulled up in front of a round, funny-looking structure. The Vargases were just beginning their family vacation. Chris, Maria, and YoYo knew they were spending it at the beach. But they didn't know where. Mr. and Mrs. Vargas had decided to surprise them about staying in a yurt in a beach state park.

"This is where we're staying," replied Mr. Vargas.

"In that thing?" exclaimed Chris. "What is it? It looks like a, a—"

"A yurt," said Maria, in a know-it-all voice.

"A what?" Chris asked.

"A yurt," Maria repeated as she climbed out of the car. "It's like a round tent, except it's sturdier because it's supported by a wooden framework inside."

"So how come you know so much about yorts?" asked Chris as he followed her out of the back seat.

"Yurts," corrected Maria. "I learned about them in school. The Mongolian people live in them, except their yurts are made out of animal skins."

"Oh, cool!" exclaimed Chris. "I hope ours is."

"Ours is made of heavy canvas," said Maria as she walked up the path to the yurt. Chris and YoYo followed close behind.

"Hey look! It has a wooden door just like a real house," said Chris. "But I can't see anything inside. He tried to peer through the window. "Maybe there are Mongolians hiding in there."

"The shade's down, Chris," said Maria. "Besides, there aren't any Mongolians around here. They live on the other side of the world. They're nomads."

"They're what?" asked Chris.

"Nomads," answered Maria. "That means they move around a lot. Instead of building a new house every time they move, they just take their yurt apart, pack it up, and take it with them!"

"But this isn't Mongo," said YoYo, tugging on Maria's pant leg. "It's the beach. So why are there yurts here?"

"So people like us can stay in them," teased Mrs. Vargas. "Some of the parks are trying them out to see if people like them."

"And they must like them," Dad joined in. "This was the last one available for this week when I made our reservation. Here's the key. Let's go check it out."

The inside of the yurt was small but cozy. A thick wooden lattice-work wall, attached to a wooden floor, supported the beige canvas walls. The top of the yurt had a round skylight that let in plenty of light. Against the far wall a small electric heater was built into a low wood wall. On the left side of the yurt was a bunk bed with a double bed on the bottom and a single bed on top. Across from it was a futon that folded down into a double bed. In between was a low wooden table.

"Oooohh, Mommy! This is so cute!" exclaimed YoYo. "But where's the bathroom?"

"It's down the path that goes right behind our yurt," said Mrs. Vargas. "I'll show you as soon as we get settled. It's for all the campers in this area. That's where the showers are too."

"Hey, can I have the top bed?" hollered Chris. "YoYo and Maria can sleep on the bottom. You and Mom can sleep on the futon."

"Sounds like you got it all figured out, Chris," said Mr. Vargas. "Is that all right with everyone else?"

"It's fine as long as YoYo doesn't start kicking me," said Maria.

"And if Maria doesn't knock me off the bed," giggled YoYo.

"Well, then let's get our stuff and get settled," said Mr. Vargas.

"So Dad, how did you decide to stay here?" asked Chris as he carried a load of stuff to the yurt.

"It was actually Mom's idea," he answered. "You know how she likes the beach. I'd read about some parks renting yurts. I thought it sounded like a fun place for us to vacation. What do you think?"

"At first I thought it was sort of weird looking," said Chris.

"You thought I'd picked some strange place to stay in that you'd be bored or embarrassed about?" Mr. Vargas asked.

"Yes, I guess I did," Chris muttered. "But now I think it's going to be great."

"It will be," replied Mr. Vargas with a twinkle in his eye. "Just trust me!"

"OK, I'll try," grinned Chris. "Say, Dad, when we get everything settled, can Maria and I do a little exploring?"

"Sure. Just don't go too far," said Mr. Vargas.

Minutes later, Chris and Maria were headed out the door of the yurt. "I wonder who's staying in that one," Maria said, pointing to the yurt next to theirs.

"I don't know," said Chris. "There doesn't seem to be anyone around right now."

"There's a car parked there," said Maria. "And look at the license plate! Someone drove a long way to get here. I wonder why? It could be a mystery!"

"Oh, come on, Maria," urged Chris. "They are probably here on vacation, just like us. There! Your mystery is solved. Let's go exploring."

As Chris and Maria walked through the campground, the main road kept going to the right, while the left branched off to a small parking area. Chris headed left. "Come on, Chris," said Maria. "That's just the RV dump area. Let's keep going."

Chris stopped for a minute and looked around. "Wait!" he said. "It looks like there's a path going up that sand dune between the trees. Let's go look!"

"Do you think it goes anywhere?" Maria asked, as she hiked up the sandy path behind Chris. "There isn't a sign post. But it looks like other people have walked here."

"Or animals," Chris said as he pushed his way past a tree limb that hung down into the path. "It could be a deer trail, or maybe a . . ."

"What is it?" exclaimed Maria, coming around the corner. "What do you see?"

"Shhhhhhh!" whispered Chris. "Take a look at this."

2

Who Is
Charles Perkins?

"What is that doing out here?" exclaimed Maria. There at the top of the small sand dune was a group of gravestones surrounded by a low iron fence. Several scrubby pine trees grew in and around the area.

"I don't know!" Chris said. "But it looks like it's been here forever!" He opened the gate and walked over to one of the gravestones. Stooping down to take a closer look, he rubbed away some of the moss and dirt with his hand. It said:

Dora Anne Simpson, Beloved Daughter,

1882-1893, Rest in peace.

Maria quickly subtracted the two dates in her head. "She was only 11 when she died," Maria said softly. She knelt beside another gravestone. "*Henry Robert Simpson, 1844-1893,*" she read. "That must have been Dora's father. And this one was her mother," she added after reading the words on a nearby headstone.

Quietly Chris and Maria continued to explore the graveyard, stopping to read the faint words carved into the old headstones. "So many in one family died around the same time," Chris said. "I wonder why? And why are they buried on top of a sand dune?"

"I'm not sure," said Maria. "But I can guess. Back in the old days, many families had their own graveyards by their houses. Maybe there used to be a home near here, but now people have forgotten about it."

"And it looks like people have forgotten about this place, too," added Chris, as he continued on up the sand dune. "Everything is overgrown and uncared for except—Maria, come here!"

Maria hurried over to where Chris was standing. There, a little farther up the hill, was one gravestone. Some weeds, recently pulled, were piled to one side. *"Charles Archibald Perkins, 1862-1907,"* Chris read from the tombstone. "Someone hasn't forgotten about him!"

Maria pointed. "And look, read what else it says. *'When safely placed upon the shore, my life was changed forever more.'* I wonder what that's all about? And who would be cleaning up his grave now?"

"It's a mystery, Maria," Chris said excitedly. "I wonder if there are any more clues around here?"

"There might be. But look at the time," said Maria, glancing at her watch. "We'd better get back to the yurt before Mom and Dad start wondering where we are."

"OK," said Chris. "I am starting to get hungry!"

"That wouldn't be anything new," teased Maria, as they headed back down the path. "I wonder who Charles Perkins was? And I'd like to learn more about this graveyard."

"We could talk to the park rangers," Chris suggested. "They might know something."

"Maybe," said Maria. "But let's go back to our yurt now."

"But there's something I'd like to know," said Chris.

"What's that?" asked Maria.

"Why isn't there a signpost at the trail? Don't you think the rangers know about the grave-yard?"

"I don't know," answered Maria. "It's not on the map we got when we came in. But how could they not know?"

When they got to the paved road, Chris and Maria stopped to empty the sand out of their shoes. As they continued walking along the road, they didn't notice a young man standing off to one side.

When Chris and Maria passed by, he turned and headed up the sandy trail they'd just come down. He continued up the trail until he reached the top of the sand dune. Removing his knap-sack, he took out a small trowel and continued the clean-up job he'd started the day before around Charles Perkins's grave.

CHAPTER

3

Trouble at the Lighthouse

"YoYo," Mrs. Vargas asked, "please help me put this tablecloth on the picnic table."

"OK, Mom!" answered YoYo, jumping up from where she'd been playing. With the tablecloth in place, Mr. Vargas set the camp stove at one end. Soon Mrs. Vargas had a pot of soup cooking. On the table were sandwiches, potato chips, and juice.

"The kids should be along pretty soon," said Mr. Vargas. "Chris's stomach always seems to know when it's time to eat!"

Minutes later, Chris and Maria came up the

path to the yurt. "Is it time for lunch?" Chris asked. "I'm starved!"

"Did your stomach tell you what time it was?" YoYo asked with a giggle.

Mrs. Vargas smiled. "Yes, we're about ready. Go wash your hands."

The Vargas family sat down at the picnic table. After a blessing, they dug into bowls of tasty soup, and yummy sandwiches.

"Anybody want to go the beach after lunch?" Mr. Vargas asked. "I heard there's an old lighthouse by the jetty."

"Cool!" exclaimed Chris. "Can we go in it?"

"I'm not sure," answered Mr. Vargas. "The lighthouse is abandoned. It hasn't been used for years."

"Sounds exciting," said Chris. "I wonder if I can climb to the top."

"I don't know, son," replied Mr. Vargas. "We'll have to see how sturdy and safe it is. Old buildings can be dangerous."

Chris rolled his eyes at Maria, then muttered, "Dad's trying to wreck my fun before it even starts. I can tell when something isn't safe."

Maria didn't answer. Instead she got up from

the picnic table and helped clear things off and put the food away.

As she and Chris were waiting for the rest of the family to get back from the restroom, a park ranger walked by. Maria suddenly remembered the questions she wanted to ask. "Excuse me, Mr. Park Ranger," she called.

"Hello," said the park ranger. "Can I help you?"

"Yes. My brother and I had a question. Actually several."

"I'll see if I have an answer," said the park ranger, smiling.

"We were exploring around, and found an old graveyard out in the woods. Do you know anything about it?" Maria asked.

"Sure do. You found the old Simpson graveyard," said the park ranger. "The Simpson family settled in this area back in the early 1800s. They used to own all this land where the park is. Their family home was near the graveyard, but it burned down many years ago. The site is now overgrown."

"But why isn't there a sign telling people where it is?" asked Chris.

"There used to be," said the ranger. "But we

were having problems with people vandalizing the graveyard and leaving trash around. So we took the sign down."

"Oh," said Maria. "That's too bad." She paused for a minute trying to decide if she should tell the ranger that someone was cleaning up one of the graves. She decided not to, so she asked, "Do you know anything about Charles Perkins?"

"Perkins," the ranger repeated as he scratched his head. "Seems like the Perkins family had something to do with the old lighthouse. In fact, one of the . . ."

"Let's go!" hollered Mr. Vargas, from the car.

"Thanks for your help," said Maria. "We gotta go!"

"I wonder what he was going to say when Dad called us," asked Chris, as they headed toward the car. "He was talking about the Perkins family."

"I don't know," said Maria. "Maybe we can talk to him again."

* * *

"Is that the lighthouse?" asked YoYo as the car pulled into the beach parking area.

"It sure is!" said Mr. Vargas.

"Wow," exclaimed Chris, as he opened the car

door. "This is awesome! It looks like it's about 90-years-old!" The lighthouse was a small, dirty-white, rectangle-shaped building built on a stone foundation. A forty-foot round tower was attached to the left side of the building. On top of the tower was a roofed lookout area and walkway where the giant light used to be.

Chris hurried up the steep cement steps into the old lighthouse. Maria and YoYo followed. Inside it was damp and dirty. A cold wind blew through the openings where windows used to be. Old boards and trash were piled in one corner. But what caught Chris's eye was the old rusty spiral stairs going up to the light tower.

"Hey, Maria!" he called. "Look at this! There are stairs going to the top."

"And they look old and ready to break," said Maria.

"Oh, they'd probably hold us. We don't weigh that much," said Chris.

"I don't know," said Maria. "It doesn't look very safe."

"It stinks in here," said YoYo as she tugged on Maria's sleeve. "Let's go to the beach."

"Chris, we're going back outside. Are you coming?" asked Maria.

"In a minute," said Chris. "I want to look around some more. Maybe I can find out more about that Perkins guy."

"OK," said Maria. "But don't do anything stupid. You know what Dad said."

"Yeah, right," muttered Chris after Maria and YoYo left the lighthouse. "You'd think I was still a baby." For a minute he stood looking up into the dim lighthouse tower. It looked like the stairs spiraled up to the top to the walkway.

I don't care what Dad says, I've just got to check this out, thought Chris. He looked quickly around the lighthouse. There was no one around. He could see Maria and YoYo outside on the jetty watching a fishing boat come into port. *Here's my chance*, he said to himself.

The first three steps were missing, so Chris grabbed the rusty railing to pull himself up. As he did there was a clunking noise, and bits of rust fell off. *Guess I'd better not stay on any of these steps too long*, Chris thought. *They might break off.*

About half way up, several more stairs were missing and Chris really stretched to make it across the gap. As he put all his weight down on the next step, he heard a noise. Then he felt the step give way.

Frantically, Chris grabbed for the rusty railing just as the step broke off from the side. He was left with only a piece of metal just big enough for the toe of his shoe to rest on. "Help!" he yelled as he dangled from the rusty railing. "Somebody help!"

But with the sound of the waves and wind, it seemed no one could hear him. Chris tried to grip the rusty metal tighter, but the weight of his body was pulling him down. He knew he couldn't hang on very much longer. And it was a long way down.

4

Angel to the Rescue

Chris closed his eyes. He tried not to think about crashing down on the hard cement floor below. *Dear God, help me not to kill myself,* Chris prayed silently. *And if I don't die, I'll really try to trust my parents more.*

Suddenly he heard a voice. "Well, well! Looks like you got yourself into a little trouble."

Opening one eye, Chris saw the tall, thin form of a young man standing below him. "Are you my angel?" Chris exclaimed.

"No," laughed the man. "But it looks like you could use one about now."

"I sure could," Chris said. "Can you help me get down?"

"I think I can figure out something," he said. "Just do what I say."

"I will," gasped Chris, as he struggled to hang on.

Within minutes, the young man had Chris down from the rusty stairs, and safely on the cement floor. "What were you doing up there?" he asked.

"Uh, I wanted to go to the top and look around," said Chris. "I wanted to see what it was like for the people who used to take care of this lighthouse."

"I see," said the man. "I imagine there's a great view from up there. But probably not worth risking your life over. Didn't you notice how rickety and old the stairs were?"

Chris looked down at his feet. "I guess I did, but I wanted to try going up them anyway," he mumbled. "I thought they'd hold me, since I'm a kid."

"Old buildings can be dangerous," said the young man.

"That's what my Dad said," muttered Chris. "But I guess I didn't trust what he said. I thought he was just trying to wreck my fun."

"Sounds like your dad wants to make sure you don't get hurt," the man said. "You would be smart to trust what he tells you. But enough scolding. I'm glad I happened to come into the lighthouse."

"So am I!" exclaimed Chris. "Thanks so much, Mister. Hey, what's your name?"

The man held out his hand for a handshake. "Perkins. John Perkins. What's yours?"

Chris shook it. "Chris. Chris Vargas. I'm here on vacation with my family."

"Sounds like fun," said John. "Well, I'm going to look around the outside of the lighthouse a bit. Enjoy your vacation, and be careful what you climb."

"I will," Chris laughed. "Thanks again, Mr. Perkins. Maybe I'll see you again."

"Maybe you will," John said as Chris turned and headed down the stairs out of the lighthouse. In the distance, he saw Maria and YoYo watching something in the water between the two jetties. Chris hurried over.

"Look!" giggled YoYo. "There's another one!"

"Another what?" asked Chris.

"Seals," said Maria. "We've been watching

them ride the waves. They are so cute." Maria turned to look at Chris. "Have you been in the lighthouse all this time? I was about ready to come looking for you."

"I've been exploring," Chris said. He shaded his eyes from the sun with his hand. "It sure is bright out here!"

"Chris, what's all over your hands?" exclaimed Maria.

Chris looked at his hands. They were the color of red bricks. "I guess it rubbed off the railings," he said.

"Railings?" asked Maria. "Were you climbing those old stairs in the lighthouse?"

Chris nodded his head. "It was a dumb idea. The stairs broke off from the wall when I was halfway up. If this guy hadn't come along— well, I hate to think what might have happened."

"How could you be so dumb?" Maria said. "But at least you didn't get hurt. Who helped you?"

"Mr. Perkins," answered Chris. "He was really nice."

"Look!" squealed YoYo. "There are two more seals!" She pointed to where two brown heads poked out above the swells in the water. "I wish I could swim with them. It would be fun!"

"Maybe it would," said Maria. "But let's get off this jetty and go over to the beach. Maybe we can find some more pretty rocks for your collection."

Chris, Maria, and YoYo walked over to the beach. They left YoYo with Mrs. Vargas and continued walking along the sand.

"I heard Dad say that sometimes you can find pieces of petrified wood washed up on the beach," said Chris. "I'd sure like to find some."

"What does it look like?" asked Maria.

"It's gray with black streaks in it, and it's really hard. If you look close you can see the wood grain," Chris said.

Before long, they stopped at a spot covered by scattered rocks. Maria bent down to pick up a small stone. "Chris," she asked, "What was that guy's name at the old lighthouse? The one who helped you?"

"John Perkins," replied Chris. "Why?"

"It's the same last name!" Maria exclaimed.

"Last name? Chris asked with a puzzled look. "What are you talking about?"

"The graveyard," Maria said excitedly.

"Perkins is the name on the gravestone—the gravestone that's being cleaned up."

Chris remembered. "That's right! The gravestone says 'Charles Perkins.' His name was John Perkins. Do you think he's the one who's cleaning it up?"

"There's only one way to find out," said Maria.

"How?"

"Let's go ask him. He still might be around the old lighthouse."

Chris and Maria turned and raced back down the beach to the jetty and out to the lighthouse. But when they got there, John Perkins was gone.

5

Lions, Panthers, and Bears!

"Oh, no!" said Maria. "He's not here!"

"It's no big deal, Maria," Chris said. "We'll probably see him again later."

"Like where?" Maria said unhappily. "There are a lot of places he could be. On the beach. At the park. It'll be like trying to find a mole in a molehill."

Chris laughed. "I don't think you're saying that right. And I don't know where we'll find him. We'll just have to keep our eyes open."

"What's that noise?" asked Maria.

"Sounds like a car horn honking," said Chris.

He looked at Maria. "That's Dad's signal for us to head to the car. We'd better hurry."

"How was everyone's day?" asked Mr. Vargas as the family settled in for the night in their yurt.

"Great!" exclaimed Chris, Maria, and YoYo.

"Are we going to the beach again tomorrow?" asked Maria.

"That depends," said Mr. Vargas.

"Depends on what?" Chris asked.

"On what you choose to do," Mr. Vargas replied with a smile. "We can go back to the beach, or we can go pet a baby bear cub."

"Pet a bear cub?" squealed Maria. "How fun!"

"Or would you prefer to hold a chocolate skunk?" Mr. Vargas teased.

"Ah, come on, Dad," scowled Chris. "There's no place around here to do that. So what are we going to do tomorrow?"

Mr. Vargas looked right at Chris as he spoke. "We're going to go to Wild Animal Park and pet a bear cub and skunk," he answered.

"You mean there really is such a place?" Chris asked.

"That's what the man I met on the beach today told me," Mr. Vargas said. "He said it's one of his kids' favorite places to go. What do you think? Should we check it out?"

"I want to go!" exclaimed Maria.

"Me too!" echoed YoYo.

"I guess I'll go too," Chris said. "I just hope that man knows what he's talking about."

The next morning the Vargas family piled into their car and headed south toward Wild Animal Park. Turning off the main road, they pulled into a dirt parking lot in front of a high wood fence. A small gift shop in front of the fence was the entrance.

"This is it?" Chris asked. "It doesn't look like much."

"The man told me it wasn't real fancy," said Mr. Vargas, "but that it was the kind of place your kids would beg to come back to."

"Looks more like I'll be begging you not to make me go," Chris replied, rolling his eyes.

Mr. Vargas ignored his comment and guided the family to the entrance. As Chris stood waiting for Mr. Vargas to purchase the tickets, he looked around the small gift shop. It was crammed with all kinds of animal souvenirs— T-shirts, stuffed animals, posters, postcards, and miniature plastic and ceramic animals.

Next to the cash register counter was a large wooden door on which the words "Enter Here," were painted.

"Today we have four-week-old baby bear cubs to pet," said the lady at the ticket counter. "And we have other animals at our *Petting Shed*. We will announce over the loudspeaker where and when to meet our animals up close. Enjoy your visit," she added with a smile as she opened the wooden door.

A short sidewalk lead to a small metal gate. Passing through the gate, they came to another gate. As Chris and Maria went through the second gate they were surrounded by bleating pygmy goats. One of the goats butted Chris's leg.

"Hey, what do you want? Is this a wild animal park or a farm?" Chris mumbled.

"I think she's hungry," giggled Maria. "She's checking to see if you have any food. See, the other people are feeding them goat feed that they bought in the gift shop. Aren't they cute?"

"Forget the goats," Chris said. "I want to find some wild animals." As Chris walked down the path he saw a chimpanzee in a huge cage beside him. It grinned at Chris, then leaped into the air and landed in a hammock.

Across from the chimp were two black panthers. "Cool!" Chris said. Then he thought *They're so close I could almost touch them. I think I'll try*. Then he noticed a sign that said KEEP FINGERS OUT OF THE CAGE.

Well, that's dumb, thought Chris. *These panthers are probably just as tame as the other animals here—only bigger*. It sure would be fun to touch one. "Here kitty, kitty," Chris called softly as he stuck his finger through the wire fence that surrounded the outside of the cage. One of the panthers looked up and started walking toward the front of the cage.

"Hey!" a voice shouted. "Get your hands out of that cage now!" Startled, Chris pulled his hand back and quickly stepped back from the cage. Chris turned to see who had yelled at him. There stood Maria, hands on her hips, staring at him.

"Chris!" she exclaimed. "What are you doing?"

"Oh, it's you," muttered Chris. "You wrecked my fun."

"Fun?" Maria sputtered. "You call sticking your hand into a panther's cage, fun?"

"Oh, they wouldn't hurt me," answered Chris. "They're probably tame."

"Tame? You don't know that, "said Maria. "Didn't you see the sign?"

"Yeah, but I . . ."

"You didn't trust what it said," Maria said. "How can you be so . . ."

"Chris! Maria!" called Mr. Vargas. "Come on back. We're going this way!" Chris and his sister ran to catch up with the rest of the family. They passed by the camels and the buffalo and a large area that held a grizzly bear.

"Now that's one big bear!" Chris said, pointing to the huge furry form sleeping in the warm sun. As the rest of the family gathered around to look, an announcement came over the loudspeaker. "Attention, park visitors. Come see and pet our lion cub, Sheba. Sheba and her trainer will be in front of the Petting Shed."

The Vargas family hurried over to where a small group of people had gathered. A man holding a big chain started to speak. "Good Morning. My name is Jim. I'm Sheba's trainer. Sheba was born and raised right here at this park. She is used to being around people, but she is still a wild animal, and she is very strong."

Maria nudged Chris. "See?"

"That is why I use a thick chain for her leash. She could easily break a leather one. Sheba is 11 months old and already weighs 90 pounds. When she is full-grown—at three years—she will weigh 350 pounds.

"Some people think Sheba looks like a big kitty. They think they can pet her like a house cat. Don't! Keep your hands away from her face. Pet her on her back. You'll be able to feel her soft fur, but won't have to worry about her snacking on any of your fingers," Jim said with a grin. "Sheba would like that, but I don't think you would! Now let's have one family at a time come up and pet Sheba. Remember, keep your hands away from her face."

"She's so soft!" exclaimed YoYo when it was their turn to pet Sheba.

"Ooooh, she is," agreed Maria. "She feels like Jenny's cat, Butterscotch."

I bet I could scratch her on the top of her head without her doing anything, Chris thought to himself. *And I'm going to do it.*

When Jim, the trainer, turned his head to

answer someone's questions, Chris quickly moved his hand to Sheba's head.

Quick as a flash, Sheba lunged at Chris's hand.

"Hey, what's going on here," Jim called, as he jerked Sheba quickly away. Sheba was upset so Jim pulled her back from the people and tried to calm her down. "Looks like someone wasn't listening to what I said. "We have rules at this park to protect our guests and our animals," he said firmly, but kindly. "We have earned the animals' trust. People need to trust the things we tell them to do, or not do."

Chris stared at the ground as the man spoke. Then he felt his father's hand on his shoulder. "Chris, I want you to stay with me the rest of the time we're here," said Mr. Vargas. "I don't think I can trust you to be off on your own."

"OK, Dad," Chris mumbled.

* * *

On the way back to their yurt, Maria and YoYo chattered excitedly about all the animals they had seen and petted—the arctic fox, the bearcat, a raccoon, a chocolate skunk, and a pair of four-week-old bear cubs.

Chris was quiet as he sat watching the scenery out the car window. When they pulled into the parking place in front of their yurt, Chris noticed someone going into the yurt next to theirs. When the man turned, Chris couldn't believe who it was.

6

More Clues

Chris nudged Maria. "Did you see that guy going into the yurt next door?"

"Yeah, sort of, why?" answered Maria.

"It's John Perkins!" said Chris.

"You mean the guy at the lighthouse?" Maria whispered.

Chris nodded his head.

Maria started climbing out of the car. "Wow, he's been right next door, and we didn't even know it. Let's go talk to him."

"Right now?" asked Chris, closing the car door. "What'll we say?"

47

"We'll ask him if he's heard of Charles Perkins," Maria decided. "And find out what he's doing here. Maybe we can find out if he knows anything about the graveyard. And then you could . . ."

"Maria," interrupted Chris. "That sounds too nosey."

"So?" Maria asked. "We've got to ask questions to solve this mystery. He doesn't have to answer them if he doesn't want to."

Chris frowned, but nodded. "I could thank him again for helping me in the lighthouse yesterday. But I don't know about just barging over there. He might not want to be bothered."

"We don't have to worry about that now," Maria said. "Here he comes out of his yurt. It looks like he's going to cook his dinner. Let's go!"

Chris and Maria walked across the small dirt path that separated their yurt from John Perkins's. As they neared the picnic table, John looked up. "Hey, it's my lighthouse buddy! How are you doing, Chris?"

"Better than the last time you saw me," Chris said with a grin. "This is my sister Maria. Maria, this is John Perkins. My friend from the lighthouse."

"Hi, John," Maria said. "Thanks for rescuing my brother from another of his crazy stunts."

"Another? Does your brother need rescuing often?" he asked with a twinkle in his eye.

"Too often," Maria answered, rolling her eyes. "He doesn't trust what Mom and Dad say. Or other grown-ups. He thinks he has to prove that they're right—or wrong."

"Sounds like my great-grandfather Charles," said John.

"Charles Perkins?" Chris asked.

"Why, yes," John answered surprised. "What do you know about him?"

"Not much, but we'd like to know more," said Maria.

"Maria and I were exploring yesterday," said Chris. "We found this old graveyard. It's full of weeds and stuff, except for . . ."

"Except for Charles Perkins's grave!" interrupted Maria. "Someone's been cleaning it. Is it you?"

John Perkins smiled. "I've been caught. I'm the one."

"But why? And why are you so far from home? And what are you doing here?" Maria's questions tumbled out of her mouth like blocks out of a bucket.

"Maria!" Chris hissed. "Don't be so snoopy!"

John laughed. "It's OK. I'm glad to have someone else interested in my quest."

"Quest?" Chris asked.

John nodded. "Yes. My quest to solve the mystery of my great-grandfather."

Maria's eyes got big. "See Chris, I told you there was a mystery."

"Hush, Maria. Let him talk," Chris said.

John laughed again. "Well, let me start at the beginning. I was working on my family genealogy for a college class. A genealogy is information about who your relatives were, where they lived, and what they did.

"My family was interesting. But what really got my attention was my great-grandfather. I'd heard a little about him growing up. But I learned a lot more as I did my research. I guess he must have been quite a handful, full of mischief, and often rather foolish.

"He also didn't like trusting his parents or their advice. But then one day something happened that caused a big change in the way he acted. I heard or read lots of rumors, but no one could tell me what had really happened. Most anyone who knew him wasn't alive anymore. I was getting information that had been passed down.

"I was curious. People didn't change like that for no reason at all. So I asked a few more questions, talked to some more people, and that brought me here."

"So that explains it!" exclaimed Maria.

"Yep!" John answered. "During my summer break from school I decided I was going to see what I could find out."

"So did Charles Perkins live around here?" Chris asked.

"He did for a while," John answered. "His father was the lighthouse keeper. They lived in a house that was across from the lighthouse."

"There used to be a house there?" Maria asked. "What happened to it?"

"When the lighthouse became automated, and didn't need a keeper, the house was left empty," John said. "Eventually, it burned to the ground. All that's left is the stone foundation, now mostly covered with sand and beach grass. You might find a few stray bricks left from the fireplace, though most of them have been hauled off."

"But the lighthouse has lasted all these years because it's made out of stone and cement," Chris guessed.

"You're right," said John. "But the lighthouse has changed some. I have pictures of what it used to look like. And that's where my search has led me."

"To the lighthouse? What do you mean?" Chris asked.

"Just before I left home, I came across some stuff that had been my great-grandfather's," John continued. "Letters he'd written and several diaries he'd kept. In one of his diaries, he had starting writing about some secret at the lighthouse, or something. Part of it didn't make any sense. It was like something was missing or he'd forgotten to write it down."

"A secret at the lighthouse!" exclaimed Chris. "How exciting!"

"It would be even more exciting if I could solve the mystery," said John. "But so far, I've found nothing. I'm running out of time. I've got to head back home at the end of this week." He paused as he dumped a can of soup into a pan. "And then there's that strange epitaph."

"Epitaph?" Chris questioned. "What's that?"

"The words that are carved on my great-grandfather's gravestone—*When safely placed upon the shore, my life was changed forever more.* He wanted that on his gravestone, but what does it mean?"

7

X Marks the Spot

"Chris," Maria asked, as they walked back to their yurt, "what do you think those words on the gravestone mean?"

"I don't know, Maria. But who cares? Forget about the eppy-hat, or whatever it's called. There's a secret in that abandoned lighthouse. Maybe even a treasure. Don't you want to find it?"

"Yes, but, I . . ." Maria started to say.

"There could be gold coins or jewels!" Chris interrupted. "Maybe Charles Perkins found a pirate's treasure washed up on shore. We could be rich! I could get a new computer. You could get a, a . . . what would you get, Maria?"

"I don't know," Maria said. "And it's crazy to even talk about it."

"Crazy! Why?" Chris sputtered.

"Because if we find a treasure, it's not ours—it's John's. He's the one who told us about it."

"I guess you're right," mumbled Chris. "So what do you want to do?"

"Find it!" exclaimed Maria. "It would still be exciting."

"Well, it's getting too late to go back to the lighthouse today," Chris said. "So let's go over all the clues we already have."

"We know that Charles Perkins's father was the lighthouse keeper," said Maria. "And that he didn't always trust what his parents said," said Chris.

Maria rolled her eyes. "Sounds like you. Maybe *you* need to be safely placed upon the shore, so you'll be changed forever more."

Chris laughed. "And that's another clue. We know Charles Perkins chose what was written on his gravestone because it says 'my' life was changed, not 'his' life."

"How could he do that if he was dead?" Maria asked.

"He told someone before he died," Chris answered.

"Oh," said Maria. "But why is he the only Perkins buried in that graveyard? It sounds like his family moved when his father wasn't the lighthouse keeper anymore."

"Maybe that park ranger we were talking to would know more," Chris suggested.

Maria nodded. "He might. Dad called us just as he was saying something about Mr. Perkins— remember?"

"I'd like to go back up to the graveyard and look around," said Chris. "Maybe we'd see something we didn't notice before."

* * *

That night Chris couldn't go to sleep. As he lay on his bunk looking out the round window at the top of the yurt, he kept thinking about everything that had happened that day. Thoughts of black panthers, Sheba, and Charles Perkins and his hidden treasure raced through his head. *Why is it so hard for me to trust Mom and Dad,* he wondered. *I want to. I try to. But then I don't. I think I need to ask*

Jesus every day to help me. Finally, when the moon was no longer overhead, Chris fell asleep.

The next morning, Chris and Maria ate big bowls of instant oatmeal for breakfast. Chris was in a hurry to ask a question. "Afer eakast kan ny . . ." he tried to say through a mouthful of mush.

"Chris," Mom interrupted, "finish swallowing your food before you talk."

Gulp! "OK, I'm done," he said a few seconds later. "What was I saying? Oh, after breakfast, can Maria and I go exploring again? We want to . . ."

Maria nudged Chris as a signal not to say anything about the graveyard. "We want to just look around the park some more," she finished.

"Can I trust you to stay out of trouble?" Mr. Vargas asked with a smile.

"I'll make sure he does," Maria replied giving Chris a light punch on his arm. "Won't I?"

Chris just grinned. After breakfast and cleanup, they headed along the road in the campground to the little sandy path to the graveyard. "I brought some paper and a pencil to take notes in case we find more clues," said

Chris as he lead the way up the path. They headed right to Charles Perkins's grave.

"Looks like John's all finished with his clean-up job," said Maria. "With the weeds and moss gone, we can see all of the gravestone."

Chris ran his hand over the front of the gravestone. "Here's something I hadn't noticed." He pointed to the lower right hand corner of the stone. "It's really faded, but I think it's a small carving of the lighthouse."

Maria knelt to look. "You're right, but it's hard to see. Didn't you bring a pencil and some paper?"

Chris shrugged. "Yes."

"I need it," said Maria.

"What for?"

Maria didn't want to argue. "Just give it to me and watch." Chris handed her the paper and Maria unfolded it and laid it across the carving of the lighthouse. Then she rubbed the lead of the pencil back and forth across the carving until an imprint of the lighthouse appeared on the paper.

Chris stared over her shoulder. "What are you doing?" he asked.

"Making a rubbing," Maria explained. "It's a

way of making a copy of the gravestone without wrecking it," said Maria. "I read about it in a book once."

Carefully Maria lifted up the rubbing. She and Chris began looking at it closely. There was an outline of the lighthouse and its stone foundation. Chris kept looking at the rubbing and then back at the gravestone. Finally he spoke. "Check this out, Maria. All of the stones in the foundation are drawn exactly alike, except for this one. If you look closely, there's a mark or line inside this one rock. Do you see it?"

Maria stared at the rubbing. Then she ran her finger over the carving on the gravestone. Suddenly she exclaimed, "That's not just a mark, it's an "X."

Chris's eyes got big. "X marks the spot! The spot where the treasure is! Let's go to the lighthouse!" He was running before he finished talking. Maria was right behind him.

CHAPTER

8

So Where Is It?

Chris and Maria didn't even stop to dump the sand out of their shoes when they got to the paved road. Instead, they hurried down the road toward their yurt. They were almost there when they ran into the park ranger.

"Are you running away from a bear?" he teased. "Or are you just in a big hurry to get someplace?"

Maria and Chris stopped to catch their breath. "Are there bears around here?" Chris asked.

"There were about 100 years ago, but not now," the ranger smiled. "So you must be in a hurry."

Chris and Maria looked at each other. "Yes, we are," said Maria. "But I'm glad we ran into you—well, almost glad!" She laughed.

"Have you been back up to the old grave-yard?" asked the park ranger.

"We were just there," Maria answered. "We had some more questions about it. The other day you started to say something about the Perkins family when our dad called us. Do you remember what you were going to say?"

The ranger scratched his head as he thought. "Let's see, the Perkins family." He paused. "Oh, yes, I was going to tell you that a John Perkins was staying in the park. He told me he was doing some research on his family in this area."

"We've met him," said Chris. "He's staying in the yurt next to ours." Chris paused for a minute trying to figure out what to say next. "Did you ever know Charles Perkins?"

The ranger laughed. "Oh, my, no. I wasn't even born yet when he lived around here."

"Oh," said Chris, his face turning red.

"But I remember my father telling me about him. The Perkins family moved away several years after the lighthouse didn't need a keeper.

Except for Charles. Seems he was sweet on one of the Simpson girls."

"Sweet on? What does that mean?" Chris asked.

"It means he was in love," Maria said with a silly-sounding voice.

"Charles married her in the big Simpson house that used to be by the graveyard," the park ranger continued. "They lived in this area for a while, and I think they had a son."

"I wonder if that was John Perkins's great-grandfather?" Maria asked.

"Could be. I don't remember his name," said the park ranger. "Then the flu epidemic came. A lot of people died, including Mrs. Perkins and some others in the Simpson family. If you look at the dates on the gravestones, you'll notice many people died around the same time."

"So, that's what happened," Maria said with a sad voice.

"It was a tragic time. My father was a small boy then, but he remembered how sad Mr. Perkins was after his wife died. He raised his boy here, but then Mr. Perkins died when he was still pretty young. Later, his son moved away from this area. And that's the last anyone has heard of them, until John showed up." He looked at his watch. "And I'd better go. I was supposed to be at someone's place ten minutes ago. See you later, kids."

"Thanks for your help," Chris said. For a moment he stood thinking about what the park ranger had told them. Then suddenly he remembered the rubbing he was holding. "The lighthouse, Maria! Let's go to the lighthouse!"

* * *

"There sure are a lot of rocks in the foundation," Maria said to Chris as they stood looking at the old abandoned lighthouse. "How are we going to have time to check everyone of them ? We're going home tomorrow."

"Be quiet, I've got to think," said Chris as he stood holding up the rubbing and looking at the lighthouse. "That's it!" he exclaimed.

"What?" Maria asked.

"You've got to be on the correct side of the lighthouse," Chris said. "So that what we see looks the same as the rubbing."

"What do you mean?" Maria asked.

"We've got to keep walking around the lighthouse," continued Chris, "until what we see looks like the picture on the gravestone."

"Oh, I get it!" exclaimed Maria. "Then we check the rocks in the foundation on that side."

As Chris held up the rubbing, he and Maria slowly moved around the area outside the lighthouse. Chris would hold up the rubbing and line it up with the lighthouse. When he could see it didn't match he would move a few feet to the right. Chris was so busy with what he was doing that he didn't notice a large signpost that he'd walked past.

"Wait a minute," Maria said. "Didn't you see the sign? It warns us to watch out for sneaker waves over where you are."

"Sneaker waves. Are those waves that are wearing tennis shoes?" Chris asked with a laugh.

"No," answered Maria. "The sign says that sometimes big waves come in unexpectedly—they sneak in. If a person isn't watching, he can be knocked into the ocean. I don't think you should go out there."

"Oh, Maria," Chris said. "It'll be fine. Besides, what if that's the spot we're looking for?"

"I don't think it's a good idea," Maria said. "The sign says the waves are the worst this time of year. We should trust what the sign says. We can check every spot but this one."

"Don't worry," Chris sneered. "If you're too afraid, I'll just go." And with that he turned and scrambled up a big boulder that was part of the jetty. "Everything will be just fine," Chris mumbled to himself. He held up the rubbing as he looked at the lighthouse from that angle. "But I'll try to keep a lookout just in case." He looked at the rubbing again. "This is almost it. Maybe if I move a little to the . . ."

"Chris, Chris, jump!" Maria screamed.

Quickly, Chris jumped off the rock and moved away from the edge of the jetty. He looked back just in time to see a huge wave come crashing down right where he'd been standing.

Maria ran over to where Chris was. "Boy, that was close," she said.

"Too close," he said wiping the salt water off his face. "I'd be soaking wet if I'd been any closer. Guess I should have trusted what the sign said."

"Guess you should have, is right," Maria said. "So after all that, was it the right angle?"

"Not quite," Chris answered. "But I think if I go a little more to the left it will be perfect." Chris and Maria moved forward and to the left several feet. Again Chris held up the rubbing.

"That's it!" exclaimed Maria. "Let's go see if we can find the rock!"

"It looks like the stone with the X is on the right and near the bottom," said Chris. "Let's look there first."

Chris and Maria ran to the outside of the lighthouse and began moving their hands over the rough rocks. They pushed and pulled trying to find a rock that might cover a hidden opening.

"We've checked every rock at least twice," Chris muttered as he gave one of them a hard kick "There's nothing here but a bunch of rocks that won't move."

Maria didn't answer. She just stared at the foundation. "Chris," she finally said, "kick that rock again."

Chris gave the rock another hard kick. As he did a section of the rock fell out, leaving a small opening. Chris looked at Maria and grinned. "I think we just found what we were looking for!"

9

Treasure Found!

Chris knelt down and started to reach his hand into the opening.

"Wait, Chris!" Maria exclaimed. "There might be a snake or spider in there." Looking around she picked up a stick of driftwood. "Here, use this to poke around in there before you stick your hand in."

Chris grabbed the stick and stuck it into the opening. He heard a thunking sound as the stick hit a metal object inside. "You hear that?" he exclaimed. "I think we've found Charles Perkins's treasure!"

71

Carefully, he used the stick to bring the object to the front of the opening. Then he reached in and brought it out. It was a small tin container, about the size of a large can of peaches. It had a lid and a small wire handle. The outside was a little rusty.

Maria jumped up and down excitedly. "We found it! We found it! Open it quick! See what's inside!"

Chris held the can in his hand. "Don't you think we should wait?"

"Wait? For what?" Maria exclaimed.

"For John Perkins," Chris answered. "You're the one who reminded me that it's his treasure. So shouldn't he open it?"

"Yahoo! Chris!" The shout made Chris and Maria both jump in surprise. After looking around wildly for a few seconds, they finally spotted John Perkins waving at them through the lighthouse window above them.

"John!" Chris yelled as he motioned with his hands. "Come see what we found!"

John hurried down the steps of the lighthouse and over to where Chris and Maria were. "What did you find? A hermit crab?"

"Nope!" Chris said with a big grin. "We found

this! We think it's your great-grandfather's."

John's mouth dropped open in surprise as he took the container from Chris. "It looks like an old round lunch pail. How did you find it?"

Chris and Maria took turns explaining how they found the clues and solved the mystery of the secret treasure. John just shook his head. "You two are amazing. I . . . I don't know what to say."

"Don't say anything," Maria said. "Just open it!"

John let out a chuckle. "I can do that!" He took out a pocketknife and began prying off the lid. Chris and Maria held their breath as he dumped the contents out onto the ground. Out tumbled three old coins, a bronze button, several agates, a small piece of painted wood, and something wrapped up in a small piece of soft cloth. John picked it up and began unwrapping it. Inside were several old pieces of paper with words hand-written on them.

"This looks like a page out of my grandfather's diary," John said. "Now I know why it didn't make sense when I read it. Some pages were missing, and here they are!"

"Can you read it? Chris said excitedly.

"I'll try." John said. "That oil-cloth protected them, but the words are really faded. And it looks like my great-grandfather didn't have the best handwriting!" After a few moments, he began to read.

I didn't think I'd ever make another entry in this diary. The sea almost got me. It's only by God's hand that I am still alive. I've gained a new respect for the sea, and for my father's advice. I am a changed lad, though no one will know this incredible story until they find these pages that I put in my secret hiding place.

Father told me to stay off the beach, but I ignored his advice, as usual. A ship had wrecked off the jetty and I wanted to see what had washed up on the beach. It was stormy and the wind was really blowing, which made the waves high. Father told me it wasn't safe to be on the beach. I thought I knew better. I didn't.

I snuck down to the beach after supper. I saw something floating in the water close to shore. I walked down to get a closer look and that's when it happened. Out of nowhere, this giant wave came down on me hard. It knocked me off my feet and swept me out into the cold dark sea. I tried to swim to shore, but it was no use. The waves were huge. The water was so cold. It made my arms and legs feel like wood. I couldn't breathe. My mouth kept filling with salt water. I knew I was going to die. The last thing I remember was saying a prayer as I drifted farther away from shore.

And then I wasn't in water. I was on the sand. Someone was calling my name, but I didn't know who it was. The voice told me to listen to my parents, that by learning to trust them, I would learn to trust God.

When I finally opened my eyes, there was no one there. I sat up to see where the voice had gone, but there were no footprints in the sand.

I know God saved me from the sea. He talked to me. I will never be the same. When safely placed upon the shore, my life was changed forever more.

Signed, Charles A. Perkins

On the back of one of the pages, Charles Perkins had listed each item that was in the container and explained why he put it there.

"Wow!" exclaimed Maria. "That's quite a story."

John nodded his head. "Yes, it is. What do you think Chris? You're sure being quiet."

Chris frowned. "Your great-grandfather sounds a lot like me. Not trusting. Thinking he knew better than adults. Maybe that's why I found this letter. To help me learn."

"Maybe you did," John said. He leaned down and picked up one of the coins. "It says on this coin, *In God We Trust*. I'd like to give this to you and Maria, for helping me. And as a reminder to trust."

"Wow! Thanks!" Maria exclaimed.

"Wow! Thanks!" echoed Chris.

"You are very welcome," said John. He handed the coin to Chris. "It's a silver dollar. You ought to be able to buy a couple of candy bars with it! So don't lose it!"

10

The Detectives Tell the Story

"Chris, please take another look around the inside of the yurt," Mr. Vargas asked. "I want to make sure we don't forget anything,"

"Sure, Dad," Chris said. Minutes later, Chris came out of the yurt carrying a small tennis shoe. "YoYo, is this yours?" He grinned as he held up the shoe. "I found it under the bed—full of rocks!"

"Oh, my shoe and pretty rocks," YoYo exclaimed. "Thanks, Chris!"

As Mr. Vargas put the last suitcase into the car, John Perkins came up the path to their yurt. "Hello!" he said. "Looks like you're leaving town,"

Mr. Vargas looked up. "Oh, hello, John. Good to see you again."

Chris and Maria looked at each other in surprise, then looked at John. "Do you know our dad?"

"Sure do!" John answered with a smile. "It's sort of hard not to bump into someone when they are staying right next to you."

Mr. Vargas closed the back of the car. "We've talked several times," he said. "When I saw John's license plate, I was curious why someone would be so far away from home. He told me he was here doing some research on his great-grandfather, and that you kids were helping."

"They've been a big help, too!" John exclaimed. "You've got a couple of great detectives! I haven't had a chance to tell you what happened." He winked at Chris and Maria. "It would be more exciting if we could show you."

"Oh, could we?" Chris and Maria said together. "Do we have time, Dad?"

Mr. Vargas looked at his watch and then at Mrs. Vargas. "I think we have time to see what our two great detectives have discovered."

"Then follow me!" Chris shouted. He led everyone down the road to the sandy path that went to the graveyard. "Well, this is where it all started," Chris said when they reached the old graveyard. "Maria and I found this place the first day we were here."

Maria spoke up. "It was all overgrown, except for one grave—Charles Perkins's. That's what started the mystery. Someone was cleaning it up, but we didn't know who, or why. After we talked to the park ranger, we learned that the graveyard belonged to the Simpson family. They used to own all this land around here."

Chris took over the story. "The ranger also told us that Charles Perkins's father was once the lighthouse keeper," added Chris. "After I met John at the lighthouse, Maria realized he had the same last name as on the gravestone. When we had a chance to talk to John, we learned that he was cleaning up the grave because it was his great-grandfather's. We also found out that he was trying to solve a mystery about the lighthouse and his great-grandfather."

Then it was Maria's turn again. "After John had the grave all cleaned up, we noticed this," she said as she pointed to the carving of the lighthouse on the gravestone. "When I made a rubbing of it, we noticed this small X."

Chris used a long pine needle to point to the faint X on the foundation. "We thought that X might mark the spot for a treasure," he added. "Just like a real treasure map!"

"So, that took us back to the lighthouse," said Maria.

"Do we have time to go there?" Chris asked Mr. Vargas.

"Of course!" said Mr. Vargas "I want to see what you found!"

"So where's the X?" asked YoYo as everyone stood looking at the old lighthouse.

Chris explained. "There isn't an X written down. It just marked where something was hidden. And that's what Maria and I had to figure out next—where that place was."

"Chris finally figured out that we needed to be on the correct side of the lighthouse," Maria said. "We needed the same side of the light-house that we could see on the rubbing."

Chris held up the rubbing so everyone could see what she was talking about. Then he led everyone over to the side of the lighthouse where they had found the treasure. "Charles Perkins hid something here," Chris said, pointing to the stone foundation. "Can you tell where?"

Mr. and Mrs. Vargas looked at each other, then shrugged their shoulders. "I think you'd better show us, Chris," laughed Mr. Vargas. "Otherwise we could be here all day!"

Chris knelt down beside the foundation and carefully removed a small piece of rock. "He hid his treasure back in this secret hiding place," he said. "It stayed there in secret for almost 100 years!"

Then John told everyone about the old lunch pail and what was inside it, including the missing pages from the old diary that solved the mystery of his great-grandfather. When he finished talking, everyone was quiet for a moment, just thinking.

Finally Chris spoke. "And that's the mystery of the abandoned lighthouse, brought to you by the great detectives, Chris and Maria!" Everyone laughed.

"Well, detectives," said Mrs. Vargas. "We've got a long trip ahead of us, so we'd better get going."

Chris stood up and brushed the sand off his

jeans. "Bye, John. Thanks for helping to make our vacation really exciting!"

"You're welcome," replied John. "And Chris?"

"Yes?"

"Keep trusting. It's a good way to stay out of trouble!"

Chris grinned. "I know."

CHAPTER

11

An Unexpected Surprise

The Shoebox was filled with excited voices when Mrs. Shue came through the doorway. Usually the kids stopped to say hello, but this morning they didn't even notice her. They were too busy listening to what Chris and Maria were saying.

Mrs. Shue stood for a moment and then cleared her throat to get their attention. It didn't work. Finally she walked over to the light switch and flipped it off.

"Hey, what's going on?" Sammy exclaimed.

"Did the power go off?" Willie asked.

"What happened to the lights?" Jenny asked.

"I turned them off!" exclaimed Mrs. Shue. "And now that I have your attention, I'll wish you a good morning and then turn the lights back on."

Mrs. Shue paused until the room was quiet. "Good Morning!" she said with a smile. Then she switched on the lights and asked, "So what's all the excitement about?"

"Chris and Maria were telling us about their vacation to the beach," said Jenny. "They found this old graveyard up on a sand dune."

"And Chris almost killed himself in a lighthouse," added Sammy. "But this guy rescued him just in time."

"And we helped the same guy solve a mystery about his great-grandfather," Maria said.

"They figured out a bunch of clues that finally led them to the old lighthouse," Willie said. "That's where they found a hidden treasure!"

"That does sound exciting," Mrs. Shue said. "So what was the mystery?"

Chris and Maria looked at each other. "Go ahead, Chris," Maria said. "You tell it."

Chris began, "Charles Perkins—that's John's

great-grandfather—was always getting into trouble. He just wouldn't listen to his parents. He didn't trust what they told him to do or not to do.

"One day there was a big change," Chris continued. "No one knew why, until Maria and I found where he'd hidden the secret."

"He wrote about it in his diary," Maria said. "But he'd torn those pages out and hidden them with some other stuff in a secret place by the lighthouse."

"When we found those pages, the mystery was solved," Chris explained. Then he told Mrs. Shue what Charles had written in the diary.

Maria finished the story. "It changed his life."

"I can see why," Mrs. Shue said. "That's quite a story. And it fits right in with our lesson this week." She turned and wrote "T-R-U-S-T" in big letters on the white board. "Sometimes it's hard to trust what our parents say," she added. "We want to find out for ourselves if what they say is right or wrong. Why can that be a problem?"

Willie raised his hand.

"Yes, Willie?"

"If my dad tells me not to go down a sidewalk

by myself in my chair because it's too steep, I need to trust him," said Willy. "If I don't, I might get hurt. Even though some hills look like they'd be fun to coast down."

Jenny spoke next. "I love cats. I'd like to pet every cat I see. But my mom tells me not to because they might scratch or bite me or be sick. Sometimes it's hard not to when I see a cute kitten. But I need to trust what my mom says."

Chris sat there for a moment and then finally raised his hand. "I almost hurt myself really bad in the lighthouse because I didn't trust what my dad said about old buildings being dangerous. And then I almost got knocked into the ocean by a wave because I didn't trust a warning sign," Chris said. "It's something I need to work on."

"And you're not the only one, Chris," said Mrs. Shue, "The Bible is filled with stories of people who had to learn to trust their parents. But because they did, they also learned to trust God. Look at Noah's sons. They grew up watching their father build a giant boat, far, far away from water, because God told him to. When they were older, they helped him build the ark. They sure needed to trust both their father and God."

She continued. "And how about Issac and Abraham, up on the mountain top with no animal for a sacrifice? That took a lot of trust for both of them. And I could tell you more stories, but I'd like you to come up with some." She smiled at her class. "I'll divide you into two teams. Let's see how many Bible characters that had to learn to trust you can find in eight minutes. You may use your Bibles."

The sound of rustling pages and low murmurs filled the room. When the time was up, Mrs. Shue asked each team to share what they had found. Soon the white board was filled with Bible names.

Maria raised her hand. "God must have known that a lot of people would have trouble with trusting because there sure are a lot of those stories in the Bible."

Mrs. Shue agreed. "Yes there are, Maria. Aren't you glad that God put them there to help us today?"

After Sabbath School, Willie came over to where Chris was standing in the hallway. "What else was in the treasure box?" Willie asked. "Was there any gold?"

Chris smiled. "There wasn't any gold, but

there were some old coins. The man gave Maria and me one for helping him."

"Really?" asked Willie. "Can I see it?"

"It's at home," said Chris. "But next time you come over, we'll look at it."

Mrs. Shue walked up. "Did I hear someone talking about old coins?"

Chris nodded. "I was telling Willie about the coin the man gave us for helping him solve the mystery."

"Do you know what kind of coin it is?" asked Mrs. Shue.

"Well," Chris answered, "I think it's a silver dollar."

Mrs. Shue's eyebrows went up. "Really? I'd like to see it. My husband and I collect old coins as a hobby."

"We'll be home tomorrow," Chris said. "Maybe you could stop by."

Mrs. Shue smiled. "I think we'll try to do that. I'll be sure to call your mother before we come."

The next afternoon, Mr. and Mrs. Shue were in the Vargases' living room looking at the old coin. After Mr. Shue studied both sides of the coin, he began looking through his book about old coins. Finally, he looked up. "Well, Chris and Maria, it looks like you have an 1859 Liberty Seated Dollar. It's in really good condition, too. Do you have any idea what it might be worth?"

Chris laughed. "Well, we know it's worth at least a dollar."

"It was back in 1859," said Mr. Shue. "Today it's worth a little bit more."

"Really?" Maria asked. "How much more?"

Mr. Shue smiled. "According to my coin guide, it's worth about $500."

Chris and Maria stared until their eyes almost popped out. Maria finally said, "Wow! That's a lot of money."

For a minute, Chris didn't say anything. Then he got a big grin on his face. "Hey, Dad, where are we going on vacation again? Maybe Maria and I can solve another mystery and earn some more money!"

"I'm not sure when or where we'll be going," his dad answered. "But treasure or not, I know you'll have fun." He grinned at Chris. "Just trust me!"

Chris grinned back. "I will, Dad. I will."

If you enjoyed this book, you'll enjoy these other Shoebox Kids adventures:

Book 1 - *The Case of the Secret Code*
    Topic: Prayer. 0-8163-1249-4
Book 2 - *The Mysterious Treasure Map*
    Topic: Baptism. 0-8163-1256-7
Book 3 - *Jenny's Cat-napped Cat*
    Topic: Forgiveness. 0-8163-1277-X
Book 4 - *The Missing Combination Mystery*
    Topic: Jealousy. 0-8163-1276-1
Book 5 - *The Broken Dozen Mystery*
    Topic: Helping others. 0-8163-1332-6
Book 6 - *The Wedding Dress Disaster*
    Topic: Commitment. 0-8163-1355-5
Book 7 - *The Clue in the Secret Passage*
    Topic: Bible. 0-8163-1386-5
Book 8 - *The Rockslide Rescue*
    Topic: Trust in God. 0-8163-1387-3
Book 9 - *The Secret of the Hidden Room*
    Topic: Prejudice. 0-8163-1682-1
Book 10 - *Adventure on Wild Horse Mountain*
    Topic: Judging Others. 0-8163-1683-X
Book 11 - *Rattlesnake River Adventure*
    Topic: Holding grudges/forgiveness. 0-8163-1757-7

$6.99US/$10.49Cdn

Order from your ABC by calling **1-800-765-6955**, or get online and shop our virtual store at **<www.adventistbookcenter.com>**.

- •Read a chapter from your favorite book
- •Order online
- •Sign up for email notices on new products

Animal Stories
the Whole Family Can Enjoy!

It all started with a perfectly pesky pet parrot named Julius, and his pal Mitch. Then came a rascally red fox, a wildly wacky raccoon, a curiously comical cow, and a thunder cat by the name of Thor! But all of them help kids celebrate God's creation with laughter and wonder. Collect the entire "herd" and get a belly laugh or two yourself from the **Julius & Friends** series.

Paperback. US$6.99, Can$9.99 each.